GEORGE AND MARTHA

The COMPLETE STORIES of TWO BEST FRIENDS

GEORGE AND MARTHA

The COMPLETE STORIES of TWO BEST FRIENDS

written and illustrated by
JAMES MARSHALL

foreword by **MAURICE SENDAK**

APPRECIATIONS BY Marc Brown, Jack Gantos, Susan Meddaugh,
Nicole Rubel, Coleen Salley, Jon Scieszka, AND David Wiesner

AFTERWORD BY Anita Silvey

HOUGHTON MIFFLIN COMPANY
BOSTON 2008

GEORGE AND MARTHA copyright © 1972 by James Marshall

GEORGE AND MARTHA ENCORE copyright © 1973 by James Marshall

GEORGE AND MARTHA RISE AND SHINE copyright © 1976 by James Marshall

GEORGE AND MARTHA ONE FINE DAY copyright © 1978 by James Marshall

GEORGE AND MARTHA TONS OF FUN copyright © 1980 by James Marshall

GEORGE AND MARTHA BACK IN TOWN copyright © 1984 by James Marshall

GEORGE AND MARTHA ROUND AND ROUND copyright © 1988 by James Marshall

Foreword copyright © 1997 by Maurice Sendak

"Wolves, Hippos, a Bathtub, and Cleveland" copyright © 2008 by Jon Scieszka

"Jimmers" copyright © 2008 by Susan Meddaugh

"Perfect and Inspiring Picture Books" copyright © 2008 by David Wiesner

"An Invitation to Tea" copyright © 2008 by Nicole Rubel

"What Would George Do?" copyright © 2008 by Jack Gantos

"A True Genius" copyright © 2008 by Marc Brown

"He Was Martha, and I Was George" copyright © 2008 by Coleen Salley

Afterword copyright © 2008 by Anita Silvey

All images for afterword provided by William Gray.

Library of Congress Cataloging-in-Publication Data is on file.

ISBN-13: 978-0-618-89195-5

Manufactured in the United States of America
DOC 10 9 8 7 6 5 4 3 2 1

DEDICATIONS

GEORGE AND MARTHA
For George and Cecille

GEORGE AND MARTHA ENCORE
For Adolph, Adrienne, Ronald, and Philip

GEORGE AND MARTHA RISE AND SHINE
For my father

GEORGE AND MARTHA ONE FINE DAY
For my nephew
Alexander Christian Schwartz

GEORGE AND MARTHA TONS OF FUN
For Maurice Sendak

GEORGE AND MARTHA BACK IN TOWN
For Rhoda Dyjak

GEORGE AND MARTHA ROUND AND ROUND
For my mother

  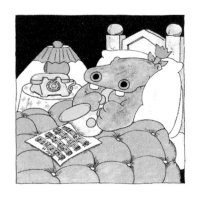

CONTENTS

Maurice Sendak

FOREWORD

THE PICTURE BOOK IS A PECULIAR ART FORM THAT THRIVES ON GENIUS, intuition, daring, and a meticulous attention to its history and its various, complex components. The picture book is a picture puzzle, badly misunderstood by critics and condescended to by far too many as mere trifle for "the kiddies." Children are routinely patronized, and thus so are we who spend our creative lives entertaining them and nourishing their spirit. Given this minefield of confusions and uncertainties, when such a work turns out looking as easy as a James Marshall picture book, it says everything about the man. Marshall is the last of a long line of masters that began in the late nineteenth century with the preeminent English illustrator Randolph Caldecott; then continued in our century with Jean de Brunhoff in France and Edward Ardizzone in England; and then via Tomi Ungerer arrived full blast in America, where the laurel wreath settled finally, splendidly, on the judicious, humane, witty, and astonishingly clever head of James Marshall.

James paid close attention to the history of his craft; he loved "the business" and brought to it all the many gifts bestowed on him—his passion for music and literature, his sly comic timing, a delicate sense of restraint and order, and that eerie instinct for just the right touch and tone. Perhaps best of all, his work was enriched by his enormous capacity for friendship. That was another gift. James the perfect friend was indistinguishable from James the perfect artist. The voice, the pulse, the heart of his words and pictures were always pure, authentic Marshall. You got the whole man.

If I remember with terrible pain my lost friend and colleague, it is only because James raised the art of friendship to an exhilarating height. I think myself the luckiest of men to have shared his sweet warmth and confidence. There is a small army of people who, I'm certain, feel the same way. He made me laugh until I cried. No one else could ever do that. He was a wicked angel and will be missed forever.

James scolded, gossiped, bitterly reproached, but always loved and forgave. All these qualities were generously funneled into his work, and there is no better example than the George and Martha books to showcase the dazzling kaleidoscope of Marshalliana. The inspiration for these two tender hippos goes back to James's shrewd appraisal of those books that most stimulated his impatient, creative intellect. He relished the extraordinary wit and brevity of the French children's books of the 1930s and the solemn, mock-serious tone of the English books of the same period. He borrowed and swiped—we all do, we all must—and it was riveting to watch James stalk, attack, and drain away the riotous madness from a favorite Tomi Ungerer and skillfully, hilariously, Marshall it.

With his first George and Martha book, James was already entirely himself. He lacked only one component in his constellation of gifts: he was uncommercial to a fault. No shticking, no nudging knowingly, no winking or pandering to the grownups at the expense of the kids. He paid the price of being maddeningly underestimated—of being dubbed "zany" (an adjective that drove him to murderous rage). And worse, as I saw it, he was dismissed as the artist who *could* do—*should* or *might* do—

worthier work if he would only dig deeper and harder. The comic note, the delicate riff, were deemed, finally, insufficient. James knew better, of course, and he was right, of course, but he suffered nevertheless. There was nothing he could do to impress the establishment; that was his triumph and his curse. Marshall *did* fulfill his genius, and its rarity and subtlety confounded the so-called critical world. The award givers were foolish enough to consider him a charming lightweight, and when Caldecott Medal time came around, they ignored him again and again.

What James couldn't know was that history was playing a nasty trick on him; "the business" was changing, seemingly overnight. The dear old cottage industry and its healthy idealism, the commingling of writer, artist, editor, production director, designer, printer, and binder, the thrumming collaboration that my generation took for granted—all gone in this new, media-bedeviled, marketing-mad Business, which has no interest in history or time for fine-grooming the fires of talent, which mindlessly shoots gifted youngsters out of the big-bucks cannon and ruthlessly lets them fall where they may. The apprenticing so critical for the development of new writers and illustrators is a thing of the past. Where, I wonder, do the new kids go, now that the old solid ground rules are corrupted and not to be trusted? It must all begin again. But history waits to be remembered, and if Marshall is, as I claim, the last of the line, then he is, too, the beginning of the next time around.

Marshall's work is undated, fresh and fragrant as a new spring garden. Nothing says this better than this edition of all thirty-five George and Martha stories. If one of James's most remarkable attributes was his genius for friendship, then George and Martha are the quintessential expression of that genius. Those dear, ditzy, down-to-earth hippos bring serious pleasure to everybody, not only to children. They are time-capsule hippos who will always remind us of a paradise in publishing and—both seriously and comically—of the true, durable meaning of friendship under the best and worst conditions.

The George and Martha books teach us nothing and everything. That is Marshall's way. Just when you are lulled by the ease of it all, he pokes you sharply. My favorite poke comes at the end of "The Surprise" in *George and Martha Round and Round*. When George has "a wicked idea" and hoses

Martha down "one late summer morning," Martha screams "Egads!" and declares war on George. Nothing he can say will soothe her wrath, but Martha suffers the consequences of her inability to forgive. She can't tell George a funny story she's read or tell him a joke she's heard because she and George are "no longer on speaking terms." But a falling autumn leaf does the trick. It's George's favorite season, so Martha goes straight to her old friend's house and they make up and watch the autumntime together. "Good friends just can't stay cross for long," George comments. "You can say that again," says Martha. A neat, sweet ending? Not a chance. Turn the page and there is a demented-looking Martha (how *did* Marshall convey dementia, malice, and get-evenness with two mere flicks of his pen for eyes?), spritzing hose in hand, lying in wait for dapper George with fedora and cane to cross her path. Marshall's last line: "But when summer rolled around again, Martha was ready and waiting."

Much has been written concerning the sheer deliciousness of Marshall's simple, elegant style. The simplicity is deceiving; there is richness of design and mastery of composition on every page. Not surprising, since James was a notorious perfectionist and endlessly redrew those "simple" pictures. The refined sensibilities of his hippos stand in touching contrast to their obvious tonnage, and his pen line—though never forgetting their impossible weight and

size—endows them with the grace and airiness of a ballerina and her cavalier. The great white splash at the end of "The High Board" in *George and Martha Back in Town* is a marvel of weight on white, with a squiggly line to delineate the shuddering catastrophe of a diving hippopotamus. Marshall says dryly: "Martha caused quite a splash."

I admit to favoring Martha; she never forgets and rarely forgives altogether, and she gets the best Marshall lines. "The Diary" from *George and Martha One Fine Day* has her toughest, yummiest exit line. In fact, that particular book showcases Martha, and we see her there at her glorious, unstable best.

Detailing the George and Martha stories, though irresistible, is certainly unnecessary. Old fans will renew acquaintance in this volume, but it is the new fans I am counting on. The hippos are charming—that's plain. The surprise will come to the young artists amid those young fans when they discover the exquisite artistry, the architecture, behind the "easy" look of it all; the quiet dignity of Marshall's work, the astonishing integration of style and form, the hint of history; the animal gestures that betray their passionate sources, opera and ballet and vaudeville and TV and movies, cartoons, paintings, travel; the gamut, simply, of the fertile genius of James Marshall.

As I write this on a lovely spring afternoon and glimpse out the window the miracle of my old weeping cherry tree cascading pink blossoms, after having spent many happy hours studying and recollecting and missing James, I am reminded of a line, now full of new meaning, from "The Last Story" in *George and Martha Encore*. Out of love for Martha, and to ease her misery over her messy garden, George stuffs store-bought tulips into the ground. Martha catches him, and George is embarrassed. But Martha is moved. "Dear George," she says. "I would much rather have a friend like you than all the gardens in the world."

Maurice Sendak
MAY 1997

Jon Scieszka

WOLVES, HIPPOS, A BATHTUB, AND CLEVELAND

I KNEW JAMES MARSHALL BEFORE I EVER MET HIM. I knew him from reading *Miss Nelson, George and Martha,* and *The Stupids* with my second-graders. We nodded when we suspected the identity of Miss Viola Swamp. We laughed when Martha clonked peeping George with her bathtub. We cracked up when Grandfather Stupid crashed through the wall to say, "This isn't heaven. This is Cleveland."

I knew Jim was smart and funny and irreverent and someone who understood the intelligence of kids. My kids' love for his stories told me so.

So when I met Jim a few years later at the Books of Wonder bookstore in New York City, I was not at all surprised to find he was—smart and funny and irreverent and someone who understood the intelligence of kids.

Jim was at Books of Wonder signing what would be one of his last books, *The Three Little Pigs.* Lane Smith and I were there signing our very first book, *The True Story of the 3 Little Pigs!*

Jim told us to stay out of the children's book business. He didn't need any more competition. I told him I was honored to meet the man who brought the Stupids to life. He said he was sorry to hear that and would look into having me banned from teaching just as soon as he could.

Jim signed his *Three Pigs* book for me, writing "For Jon—A Rising Star." Lane and I signed our *True Story* for him, writing, "Jim—take a look at the TRUE story." And Lane drew a picture of A. Wolf, with a tiny bit of blood dripping from his smile . . . and an exactly A. Wolf–sized bite missing out of Martha's plump hippo shoulder in front of him.

I had planned to run into Jim plenty more times to tell him how his stories had inspired me to truly trust kids and respect their sense of humor.

But that was the first and last time I saw Jim.

I never had a chance to tell him how his books made possible a smooth-talking wolf and little man made of stinky cheese. But the good news is that we all still have those James Marshall worlds where we can nod to Viola Swamp, laugh with Martha, crack up at Grandfather Stupid, and meet Jim . . . in heaven, or in Cleveland.

Jacket art © 1992 by Lane Smith

Jacket art © 2005 by Lane Smith

JON SCIESZKA is a former elementary school teacher turned award-winning author, and the founder of the Guys Read website. After earning his master's degree in fiction writing from Columbia University, he went on to write such books for children as Math Curse, The Stinky Cheese Man, The True Story of the 3 Little Pigs!, *and* Squids Will Be Squids, *all illustrated by his friend and frequent collaborator, Lane Smith. Born in Flint, Michigan, he now lives in Brooklyn, New York.*

Five
Stories About
Two Great
Friends

Story
Number
One

Split Pea Soup

Martha was very fond of making split pea soup.
Sometimes she made it all day long. Pots and pots of
split pea soup.

If there was one thing that George was *not* fond of, it was split pea soup. As a matter of fact, George hated split pea soup more than anything else in the world. But it was so hard to tell Martha.

One day after George had eaten ten bowls of
Martha's soup, he said to himself, "I just can't stand
another bowl. Not even another spoonful."
So, while Martha was out in the kitchen,
George carefully poured the rest of his soup into his
loafers under the table. "Now she will think I have
eaten it."
But Martha was watching from the kitchen.

"How do you expect to walk home with your loafers full of split pea soup?" she asked George.

"Oh dear," said George. "You saw me."

"And why didn't you tell me that you hate my split pea soup?"

"I didn't want to hurt your feelings," said George.

"That's silly," said Martha. "Friends should always tell each other the truth. As a matter of fact, I don't like split pea soup very much myself. I only like to make it. From now on, you'll never have to eat that awful soup again."

"What a relief!" George sighed.

"Would you like some chocolate chip cookies instead?" asked Martha.

"Oh, that would be lovely," said George.

"Then you shall have them," said his friend.

STORY NUMBER TWO

The Flying Machine

"I'm going to be the first of my species to fly!" said George.

"Then why aren't you flying?" asked Martha. "It seems to me that you are still on the ground."

"You are right," said George. "I don't seem to be going anywhere at all."

"Maybe the basket is too heavy," said Martha.

"Yes," said George, "I think you are right again.
Maybe if I climb out, the basket will be lighter."

"Oh dear!" cried George. "Now what have I done? There goes my flying machine!"

"That's all right," said Martha. "I would rather have you down here with me."

The Tub

STORY NUMBER
THREE

George was fond of peeking in windows.

One day George peeked in on Martha.

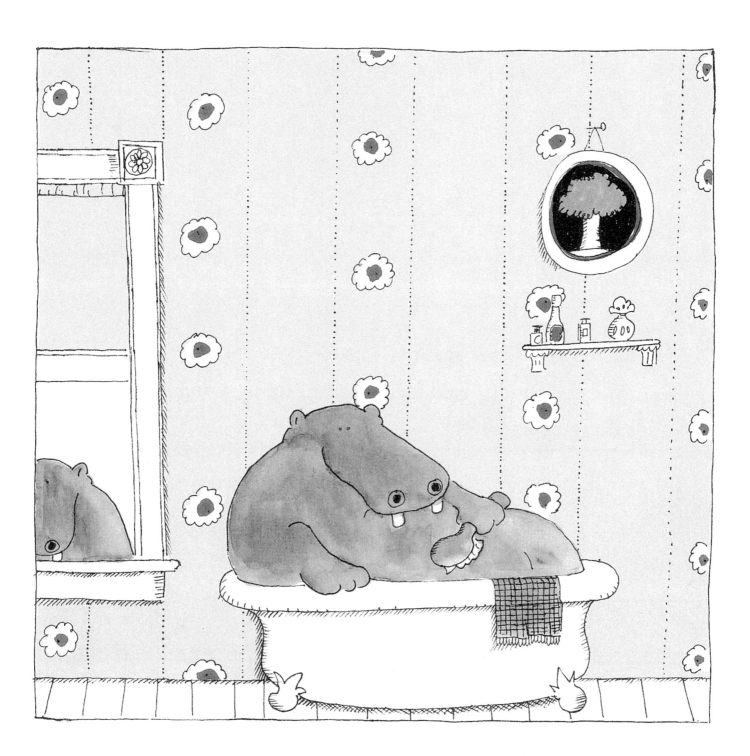

He never did *that* again.

"We are friends," said Martha. "But there is such a thing as privacy!"

STORY NUMBER FOUR

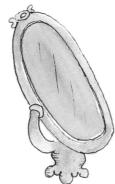

The Mirror

"How I love to look at myself in the mirror," said Martha.

Every chance she got, Martha looked at herself in the mirror.

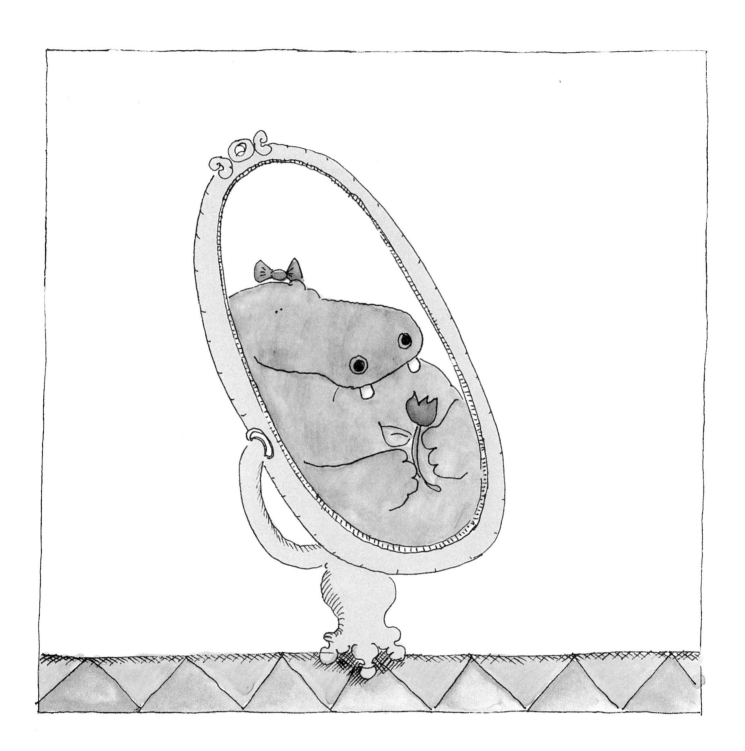

Sometimes Martha even woke up during the night to look at herself.

"This is fun." She giggled.

But George was getting tired of watching Martha
look at herself in the mirror.

One day George pasted a silly picture he had drawn
of Martha onto the mirror.

What a scare it gave Martha. "Oh dear!" she cried.
"What has happened to me?"

"That's what happens when you look at yourself
too much in the mirror," said George.

"Then I won't do it ever again," said Martha.
And she didn't.

THE LAST STORY

STORY

The Tooth

One day when George was skating to Martha's house, he tripped and fell. And he broke off his right front tooth. His favorite tooth too.

When he got to Martha's, George cried his
eyes out.

"Oh dear me!" he cried. "I look so funny without
my favorite tooth!"

"There, there," said Martha.

The next day George went to the dentist.

The dentist replaced George's missing tooth with a lovely gold one.

When Martha saw George's lovely new golden tooth, she was very happy. "George!" she exclaimed. "You look so handsome and distinguished with your new tooth!"

And George was happy too. "That's what friends are for," he said. "They always look on the bright side and they always know how to cheer you up."

"But they also tell you the truth," said Martha with a smile.

Susan Meddaugh

JIMMERS

I HAVE A FRAMED PIECE OF JIM MARSHALL'S ART HANGING IN MY KITCHEN. It's a wonderful drawing and on the back it's covered with Jim's dedications: "For Devine Susan Meddaugh, From Thoughtful Jim Marshall," "For Good Old Susan, From Handsome Jim Marshall," "For Ms. Meddaugh, From Mr. Marshall," and more, all crossed out. Then, down in the corner, he wrote: "To Susan, From Jimmers."

I was one of the lucky ones who worked at Houghton Mifflin when Jim did his first books, *Plink, Plink, Plink,* and then the George and Martha stories. I think everyone in the department considered him a friend. I'd start to smile the moment he got off the elevator.

Then he would read a new story. I can hear him as George, and then as Martha. I hear him as Viola Swamp and Miss Nelson. I hear him as Eugene the turtle and Emily Pig. And you can see Eugene and Emily waiting in the wings in "The Amusement Park" in *George and Martha One Fine Day.*

When I left Houghton to do my own work, Jim found me an apartment in Charlestown, right above his. As such, he was able to monitor my life, make observations, give advice and encouragement—some of it helpful. And of course entertain me with stories of his latest adventures. I loved how he lived his life. I miss him.

But I can still clearly hear his voice when I read his books. I can still hear him when I see his pictures, or come upon the occasional postcards he sent from London or Paris—the best kind of postcards with drawings and brief messages, usually about eating too much or the high price of hotel rooms.

Once, when asked to do a brief autobiography for Houghton, Jim wrote something called "Down and Out in Rio." Total fiction, I believe, but outrageously funny. That was Jim to the core. He was a combination of all the fabulous characters he created. And an artist of incomparable talent.

Jacket art © 1992 by Susan Meddaugh   Jacket art © 2004 by Susan Meddaugh

SUSAN MEDDAUGH worked at Houghton Mifflin for ten years as a designer, art editor, and art director before she decided to strike out on her own as a children's book illustrator. Since that time, she has written and illustrated many popular books for children, including several about Martha, the alphabet soup–eating, talking dog. Her work has been honored with a New York Times Best Illustrated Book Award and the New England Book Award. She lives in Sherborn, Massachusetts.

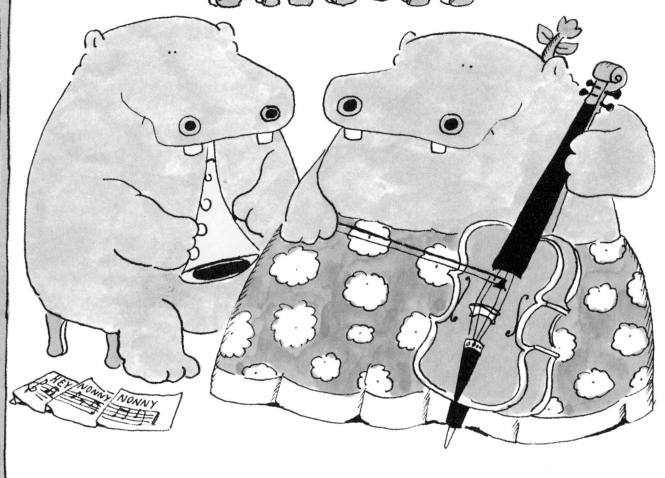

MORE STORIES ABOUT TWO GREAT CHUMS

~

STORY NUMBER ONE

THE DANCE RECITAL

George and Martha were having a disagreement.

"I think dancing is dumb," said George.

"Dancing is not dumb!" exclaimed Martha.

"Dancing is fun! And if you don't come to my dance recital, I'll be very angry!"

So, of course, George went to Martha's recital.

"I'm going to hate this," he said to himself.

But what a surprise for George!

Martha's Dance of the Happy Butterfly was so impressive.

"Dancing looks like fun," said George.

The next day George went to dancing class.

"You see," said Martha, "dancing is fun!"

Very soon George was in his own dance recital.
Martha said that his Mexican Hat Dance was the
best she had ever seen.

THE SECOND STORY

THE FRENCH LESSON

George went to Martha's house for his French lesson.

"Bonjour, Martha," said George.

"Bonjour, George," said Martha.

George sat next to Martha on the sofa.

"How do you say 'Give me a kiss' in French?"
asked George.

"You say 'Voulez-vous m'embrasser?' "*
answered Martha.

*(This sounds like "Voo-lay-voo mom-brass-ay?")

And that is just what George did.

"Tee-hee," said Martha.

"I knew you were going to do that."

STORY NUMBER THREE

THE DISGUISE

George decided to dress up as an Indian.

"This disguise will really fool Martha," he chuckled.

"She'll never recognize me."

But Martha wasn't fooled a bit.

"Hi, George," she said.

"Why are you wearing that Indian costume?"

George was so disappointed.

He walked away hanging his head.

Martha felt simply awful.

She hadn't meant to hurt George's feelings.

"George," said Martha. "I would never have recognized you if it hadn't been for your bright smiling eyes. It's so hard to disguise smiling eyes." And, of course, George felt much, much better.

STORY NUMBER FOUR

THE BEACH

One day George and Martha went to the beach.

"I love the beach!" exclaimed Martha.

"So do I," said George.

"However, we must be sure to put on our suntan lotion."

But Martha refused to put on her suntan lotion.

"You'll be sorry," George called out.

"Oh, pooh," said his friend.

"You're a fuss-budget, George."

Martha was having such a lovely time.

The next day Martha had a terrible sunburn!

She felt all hot and itchy.

But George never said "I told you so."

Because that's not what friends are for.

THE LAST STORY

STORY

THE GARDEN

Martha was so discouraged.

Her garden was an ugly mess of weeds.

"I just don't seem to have a green thumb," she sobbed.

George hated to see Martha unhappy.

He wanted so much to help.

Suddenly George had a splendid idea.

He went to the florist and bought

all the tulips in the shop.

Tulips were Martha's favorite flowers.

Very quietly George crept into Martha's garden
and stuck the tulips in the ground.
But just then Martha happened to look out the
window.

"Oh, dear," said George.

"You're always catching me."

But Martha was so pleased.

"Dear George," she said.

"I would much rather have a friend like you

than all the gardens in the world."

David Wiesner

PERFECT AND INSPIRING PICTURE BOOKS

I FIRST MET JIM MARSHALL IN JUNE OF 1989 at the American Library Association Convention when Jim, Jerry Pinkney, Allen Say, and I all had titles that were named Caldecott Honor Books. The moment you met Jim you felt as if you had known him forever because he was so funny and so welcoming. I then saw him a few months later at a book fair in Providence, Rhode Island. Chris Van Allsburg, David Macaulay, Maurice Sendak, and Jim were all there . . . and me. I kept wondering what I was doing there, because they were so much better known than I was. But Jim kept insisting that I was one of the gang. He treated me as if I belonged. As soon as he found out that my wife, Kim, was a surgeon, he said, "Oh, wonderful. I have all these medical things that I'd love to talk about." In the end I had a delightful time, in large part because of Jim.

I didn't fully appreciate his books, however, until I was reading them aloud to my son Kevin. I found them immediately engaging and funny. I remember stopping in the middle of a George and Martha book and saying, "I can't believe how incredibly good this is." It is so hard to create a book that deceptively simple in both writing and art. I then sat down and went through his George and Martha books and the Stupids saga, asking myself, "How did he do this?" Both text and pictures had this perfect note of humor that was awe-inspiring. Nothing extraneous exists in the stories; he has stripped everything away to get the essence of storytelling pictures and words. You wouldn't want to add anything or take anything away. It is all necessary and perfect.

A few years ago, David Macaulay showed me a sublime little Ernest Shepard drawing that he has in his studio. Along with it David displayed the preparatory sketches. It was fascinating to look at those sketches; you could see that Shepard went in and picked out just the lines that he wanted. Clearly a backlog of work had gone into making the final drawing look effortless. I learned that it was the same with Jim; a lot of work preceded the final picture. His artwork may look effortless, but it was a lot harder to do than anyone can imagine.

In my own books I am often working with complicated ideas. But as I develop them, I keep thinking of the artists who manage an economy of text and line. I keep trying to convey my material with fewer words or pictures. Or say it as clearly and cleanly as Jim Marshall. Jim's aesthetic is one I completely admire. He is one of a small group of people whose work I always think about when I am trying to tell a story.

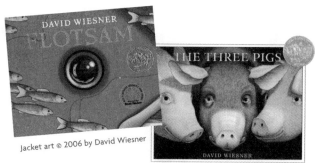

Jacket art © 2006 by David Wiesner

Jacket art © 2001 by David Wiesner

DAVID WIESNER has won the prestigious Caldecott Medal three times—for Tuesday, The Three Pigs, *and most recently,* Flotsam. *His work has also been honored with numerous other awards. As a child with an active imagination, he drew pictures and stories from a young age. After attending the Rhode Island School of Design, he committed himself to his own special brand of storytelling. He lives in Pennsylvania with his wife and children.*

One day George wanted to impress Martha.

"I used to be a champion jumper," he said.

Martha raised an eyebrow.

"And," said George, "I used to be a wicked pirate."

"Hmmm," said Martha.

George tried harder. "Once I was even
a famous snake charmer!"

"Oh, goody," said Martha.

Martha went to the closet and got out Sam.

"Here's a snake for you to charm."

"Eeeek," cried George.

And he jumped right out of his chair.

"It's only a toy *stuffed* snake," said Martha. "I'm surprised a famous snake charmer is such a scaredy-cat."

"I told some fibs," said George.

"For shame," said Martha.

"But you can see what a good jumper I am," said George.

"That's true," said Martha.

Martha was in her laboratory.

"What are you doing?" asked George.

"I'm studying fleas," said Martha.

"Cute little critters," said George.

"You don't understand," said Martha.

"This is serious. This is science."

The next day, George noticed that Martha was scratching a lot. She looked uncomfortable.

George bought Martha some special soap. After her shower Martha felt much better.

"I think I'll stop studying fleas," said Martha.

"Good idea," said George.

"I think I'll study bees instead," said Martha.

"Oh dear," said George.

STORY NUMBER 3

THE PICNIC

One Saturday morning, George wanted to sleep late.

"I love sleeping late," said George.

But Martha had other ideas.

She wanted to go on a picnic.

"Here she comes!" said George to himself.

Martha did her best to get George out of bed.

"Picnic time!" sang Martha.

But George didn't budge.

Martha played a tune on her saxophone.

George put little balls of cotton in his ears and pulled up the covers.

Martha tickled George's toes.

"Stop it!" said George.

"Picnic time!" sang Martha.

"But I'm *not* going on a picnic!" said George.

"Oh yes you *are!*" said his friend.

Martha had a clever idea.

"This is such hard work," she said, huffing and puffing.

"But I'm not going to help," said George.

"I'm getting tired," said Martha.

George had fun on the picnic.

"I'm so glad we came," said George.

But Martha wasn't listening.

She had fallen asleep.

Martha was nervous.

"I've never been to a scary movie before."

"Silly goose," said George. "*Everyone* likes scary movies."

"I hope I don't faint," said Martha.

Martha *liked* the scary movie. "This is fun," she giggled.

Martha noticed that George was hiding under his seat.

"I'm looking for my glasses," said George.

"You don't wear glasses," said Martha.

When the movie was over, George was as white as a sheet.
"Hold my hand," George said to Martha. "I don't
want you to be afraid walking home."
"Thank you," said Martha.

"Where are you going, George?" asked Martha.

"I'm going to my secret club," said George.

"I'll come along," said Martha.

"Oh no," said George, "it's a secret club."

"But you can let *me* in," said Martha.

"No I can't," said George. And he went on his way.

Martha was furious.

When George was inside his secret clubhouse, Martha
made a terrible fuss.

"You let me in," she shouted.

"No," said George.

"Yes, yes," cried Martha.

"No, no," said George.

"I'm coming in whether you like it or *not!*" cried Martha.

When Martha saw the inside of George's clubhouse,
she was so ashamed.

"You old sweetheart," she said to George.

George smiled. "I hope you've learned your lesson."

"I certainly have," said his friend.

Nicole Rubel

AN INVITATION TO TEA

IN 1975 I WAS ATTENDING THE BOSTON MUSEUM SCHOOL OF FINE ARTS. During my last semester, my teacher asked our class to draw one object over and over for three weeks. I drew my goldfish in a series of colorful and bold pastels. Then I was given a new assignment; my teacher wanted me to go to a bookstore and look at children's book illustrations.

"I'm a fine artist, not an illustrator," I protested. In my mind the word *illustrator* indicated someone who drew either cute art or realistic watercolors. I didn't see how it fit me. My wise teacher smiled like a Cheshire cat and said, "Go!"

The next day I wandered over to the children's section of the Harvard Bookstore. I picked up a few books and shook my head. Then I saw *George and Martha* peeking up at me. I saw two hippos arguing over a bowl of pea soup. George poured it into his shoes instead of eating it. I started laughing. The artwork was simple, bold, and funny—unlike anything I had ever seen. It was magical! A giant light bulb flashed inside my head. I knew right then, in the bookstore, I wanted to make children's books for the rest of my life, and I've never thought otherwise.

I bought the book and showed it to Jack Gantos, then a writing major at Emerson College. "Look at this!" I exclaimed. He agreed that *George and Martha* was wonderful!

"Who is James Marshall?" I wondered. Then I did something odd. I opened a Boston phonebook, looked him up, and called. I don't know why I did this, because thirty years ago I was the shyest person in the world. Marshall answered the phone, and I explained I was an art student in love with his work. He did something amazing. He invited me and Jack to tea!

A few days later Jack and I arrived at his apartment. Instantly we were charmed. His rooms were full of neat things from Texas, and when we looked out his window we saw the Bunker Hill Monument, present in so many of his pictures.

Jim was warm, funny, and sincerely interested in my artwork. He flipped through my portfolio and said, "You are really talented, Nicole. Your artwork is original. You should and will get published in children's books. I'm sure of it. Call Walter Lorraine at Houghton Mifflin and show him your work. But remember . . . please don't mention my name because Walter likes to discover his own talent."

Just as Jim predicted, Walter Lorraine wanted my artwork. More than thirty years later, I still thank George and Martha and Jim Marshall for my wonderful career.

Jacket art © 2006 by Nicole Rubel

Jacket art © 1997 by Nicole Rubel

NICOLE RUBEL is an award-winning author and illustrator. She has a degree in fine arts from the Boston Museum School and has taught ceramics, silk screening, and mural design to children. Booklist has described her artwork as "busy, brightly colored paintings, done in child appealing primitive style, filled with subtle, humorous touches." She has more than sixty picture books to her credit, including the popular Rotten Ralph series, and her first novel, It's Hot and Cold in Miami. She currently resides with her husband on a farm in Aurora, Oregon, with a Siamese cat named Cougar, a corgi named Fang, two horses, and two sheep.

One morning when George looked out his window,

he could scarcely believe his eyes.

Martha was walking a tightrope.

"My stars!" cried George. "I could *never* do that!"

"Why not?" said Martha. "It's tons of fun."

"But it's so high up," said George.

"Yes," said Martha.

"And it's such a long way down," said George.

"That's very true," said Martha.

"It would be quite a fall," said George.

"I see what you mean," said Martha.

Suddenly Martha felt uncomfortable.

For some reason she had lost all her confidence.

She began to wobble.

George realized his mistake.

Now he had to do some fast talking.

"Of course," he said, "anyone can see you love walking the tightrope."

"Oh, yes?" said Martha.

"Certainly," said George. "And if you love what you do, you'll be very good at it too."

Martha's confidence was restored.

"Watch this!" she said. Martha did some fancy footwork on her tightrope.

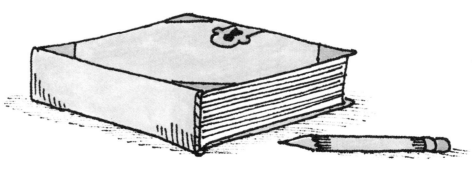

Whenever Martha sat down to write in her diary, George was always nearby.

"Yes, George?" said Martha.

"I was just on my way to the kitchen," said George.

"Hum," said Martha.

Martha decided to finish writing outdoors.

"How peculiar," she said to herself. "I can still smell George's cologne."

Then Martha heard leaves rustling above her.

"Aha!" she cried. "You were spying on me!"

"I wanted to see what you were writing in your diary," said George.

"Then you should have asked my permission," said Martha.

"May I peek in your diary?" asked George politely.

"No," said Martha.

STORY NUMBER THREE

THE ICKY STORY

At lunch George started to tell an icky story.

Martha strongly objected.

"Please, have some consideration," she said.

But George told his icky story nevertheless.

"You're asking for it," said Martha.

When Martha finished her lunch, *she* told an
icky story. It was so icky that George felt all queasy
inside. He couldn't even eat his dessert.

"You're the champ," said George.

"Don't make me do it again," said Martha.

"I won't," said George.

STORY NUMBER FOUR

THE BIG SCARE

"Boo!" cried George.

"Have mercy!" screamed Martha.

Martha and her stamp collection went flying.

"I'm sorry," said George. "I was feeling wicked."

"Well," said Martha. "Now it's my turn."

"Go ahead," said George.

"Not right away," said Martha slyly.

Suddenly George found it very difficult to concentrate on what he was doing.

"Any minute now, Martha is going to scare the pants off me," he said to himself.

"Maybe she is hiding someplace," he said.

George made sure that Martha wasn't hiding under the sink.

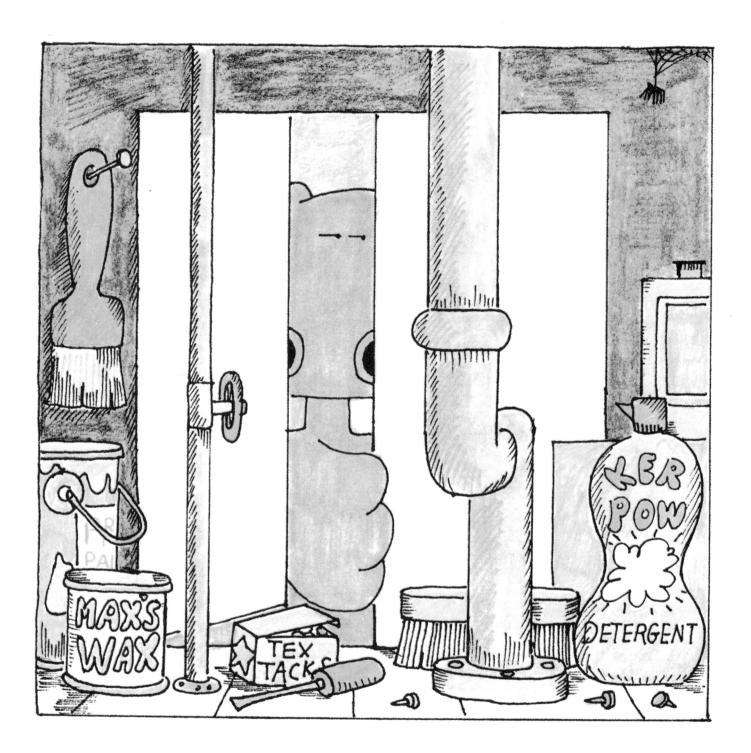

During the day George

got more and more nervous.

"Any minute now," he said.

But Martha was relaxing in her hammock.

"I'm sorry I forgot to scare you," said Martha.

"That's all right," said George. "It wouldn't have worked anyway. I'm not easily frightened."

"I know," said Martha.

THE LAST STORY

THE AMUSEMENT PARK

That evening George and Martha
went to the amusement park.
They rode the ferris wheel.

They rode the roller coaster.

They rode the bump cars.

They were having a wonderful time.

But in the Tunnel of Love, Martha

sat very quiet.

It was very very dark in there.

Suddenly Martha cried "Boo!"

"Have mercy!" screamed George.

"I didn't forget after all," said Martha.

"So I see," said George.

Jack Gantos
WHAT WOULD GEORGE DO?

I MET JIM MARSHALL WHEN NICOLE RUBEL AND I WERE TRYING TO FIGURE OUT HOW TO PUT TOGETHER A GOOD PICTURE BOOK. I was writing some fairly dull stories, and she was well ahead of me with her illustrations. We knew we needed some advice. Nicole had seen the George and Martha books and loved Jim's art, and I had read *The Stupids Step Out*, which made me feel liberated to write *anything*. Nicole looked him up in the telephone book and called him, and he was polite enough to invite us over to his place in Charlestown, across the river from Boston.

He lived near the very steep top of Bunker Hill, which was crowned with the Bunker Hill Monument. Nicole and I hiked up the uneven red brick sidewalk and were breathless when we arrived. Jim greeted us warmly and quickly offered us something to drink. Nicole remembers that Jim served us tea, but I distinctly remember that he offered me a scotch and I quickly accepted. When he returned from the kitchen, he handed me an eight-ounce tumbler filled to the brim. He was not only polite but generous.

Perhaps I should have had tea or a glass of water, because I was very thirsty. As Jim showed us his art and talked about publishing and manuscript preparation, I steadily sipped on the tumbler of scotch until it was finished. We were there for quite some time and Jim probably thought he had done his duty as a teacher. But, because he was from Texas and so polite, he offered us one more drink. Nicole declined. She was from Florida and knew the offer was simply good manners on Jim's part. But I said, "Sure!" and held out my glass. Jim retreated to the kitchen and when he returned gave me a second tumbler of scotch filled to the brim. I took one sip when I realized I was supposed to have used my manners and graciously declined the drink and left.

At my first opportunity I slipped the tumbler onto a windowsill and slid it behind a curtain. I felt a little like George when he poured his pea soup into his loafer. And then we left.

Sometime after Nicole and I had taken Jim's advice and published *Rotten Ralph* with Houghton Mifflin, Anita Silvey, who was the director of marketing, arranged for a book signing at a department store in Hartford, Connecticut. Anita drove Nicole and me down and Jim was supposed to meet us there.

We arrived on time. Jim was not there, and so we made small talk with the book buyers and sellers and waited. Everyone was getting a little nervous because a few people had gathered, purchased books, and were eager to have them signed. Finally, the manager of the book department was called to the telephone. A minute later he returned and informed us that Jim couldn't make it. "He has broken his leg while jogging," the manager said. "I was told it was a *terrible* fall."

We were all quite upset. Jim hadn't said he was a jogger, but he was in good trim and I figured he might have slipped or tripped on that treacherously steep sidewalk on Bunker Hill.

The book signing soon began. Anita offered to have autographed bookplates sent to those who purchased Jim's books. That cheered his fans, but as I looked down at my hand with a pen in it, I hoped Jim had not hurt his.

A few weeks later I was walking through the Houghton Mifflin lobby at #2 Park Street when suddenly Jim came bounding down the steps without any evidence of a broken leg. I desperately wanted to say something about his rapid recovery, but he had been so polite to me, I just checked my thoughts.

"How was the event in Hartford?" he asked when he spotted me.

"Great," I said, fibbing a bit. I had really missed seeing him.

"Sorry I couldn't make it," he added. "Had a bad case of the flu."

I just smiled to myself and wished him well. After all, that's what George would have done for Martha, or Martha for George.

Jacket art © 2007 by Beata Szpura

Jacket art © 1976 by Nicole Rubel

JACK GANTOS spent his childhood reading, and spends his adulthood writing. The author of numerous books for children, young adults, and adults—including the Rotten Ralph series and Joey Pigza novels—he helped develop the master's degree programs in children's book writing and literature at Emerson College and at Vermont College. His books have won many awards and have been named Newbury Honor and Printz Honor books. He lives and works in Boston, Massachusetts.

FIVE STORIES ABOUT THE BEST OF FRIENDS

STORY NUMBER ONE

THE MISUNDERSTANDING

George was practicing his handstands.

"This calls for concentration," he said.

Suddenly the doorbell rang.

It was Martha.

"I've come to chat," she said.

"Not this afternoon," said George. "I want to be alone."

"I hope Martha understands," said George.

But Martha did not understand.

Martha was offended.

Martha was hurt.

And Martha was *mad!*

A few minutes later, George's telephone rang.

It was Martha.

"George," she said, "I never want to see you again!"

And she slammed down the receiver.

"Oh dear," said George.

Martha was mad all afternoon and evening.

Finally she got out her saxophone.

"This will calm me down," she said.

Soon Martha was having quite a bit of fun.

In fact she was having *so* much fun that she didn't even answer her telephone.

"Oh dear," said George. "Martha must still be upset."

But Martha had forgotten all about the misunderstanding.

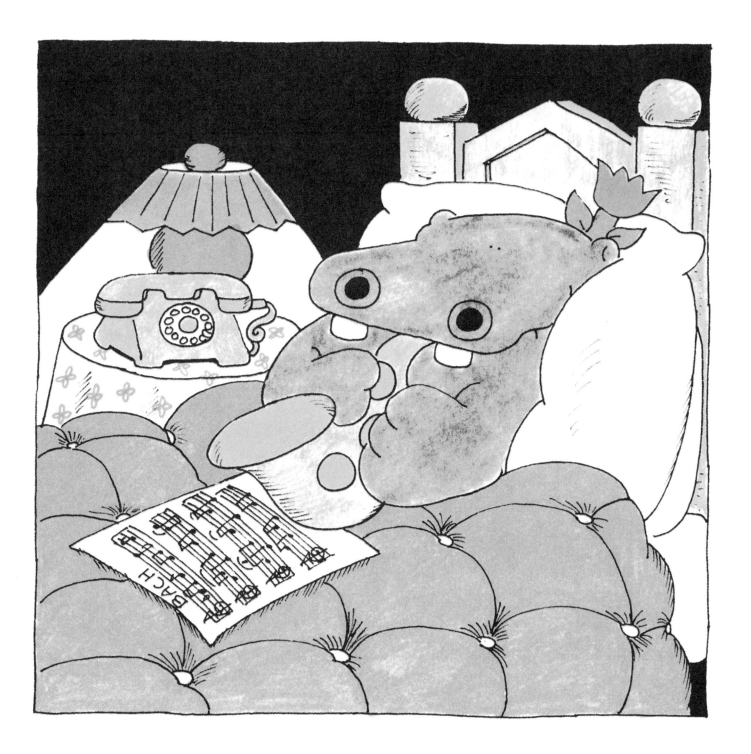

George had a sweet tooth.

He just couldn't stop himself from eating sweets.

"You know what they say about too much sugar," said Martha.

"Let's not discuss it," said George.

Late at night George would raid the refrigerator to satisfy his sweet tooth.

"You'll weigh a ton," said Martha.

"Let's not discuss it," said George.

"This calls for action!" said Martha.

And she lighted up a cigar.

"Stop that!" cried George. "You'll make yourself sick!"

"Let's not discuss it," said Martha.

"You'll ruin your teeth!" cried George.

"We won't discuss it," said Martha.

"Please!!" cried George. "You're ruining your health."

"No discussion," said Martha.

Martha began to turn a peculiar color.

George couldn't stand it any longer,

and he fell to his knees.

"I'll do anything you say!" he begged.

"Will you cut down on your sweets?"

said Martha.

"I promise," said George.

And Martha put out her cigar.

One day Martha stepped into a
photography booth.
"I love to have my picture taken,"
she said.
"Click," went the camera.

When Martha saw her photograph,

she was thrilled.

"I've never looked prettier," she said.

George was trying to hypnotize Martha.

"Your eyes are getting heavy," said George.

"I believe they are," said Martha.

"You are getting sleepy," said George.

"That's true," said Martha.

And in a moment Martha seemed sound asleep.

"Success!" whispered George.

Ever so quietly George tiptoed to the kitchen,
where he kept his cookie jar.

"Ah-ha!" cried Martha.

George was ashamed.

He'd broken his promise.

"Would you like a cookie?" he asked Martha.

"Yes, I would!" she said.

And she ate them all.

It was George's birthday, and Martha
stopped by the bookshop to buy a gift.
"He loves to read," Martha told the
salesperson.

On the way to George's house,
Martha played a tricky game of
hopscotch.

George could hardly wait for his gift.

"I can't stand the suspense," he said.

But when Martha went to look for George's

book, it wasn't there.

"I'm waiting," said George.

"What will I do?" said Martha to herself.

"I'm waiting," said George.

Martha quickly decided to give George

the photograph of herself.

"It's not much," she said.

When George saw Martha's picture,

he fell off his chair laughing.

"Well!" said Martha. "What's so funny?"

"This is the best gift I've ever received,"
said George.

"It *is?*" said Martha.

"Of course," said George. "It's wonderful to have
a friend who knows how to make you laugh."
Martha decided to swallow her pride.
She saw that the photograph was pretty funny
after all.

Marc Brown

A TRUE GENIUS

MY FIRST ENCOUNTER WITH JIM MARSHALL WAS AT A SMALL BOOKSTORE ON BEACON HILL IN BOSTON. My first book, *Arthur's Nose,* had just been published by the Atlantic Monthly Press. Jim had become an overnight star with the appearance of his first George and Martha book. Gene Shalit was raving about it on *The Today Show*. In our business at that time, to be recognized on *The Today Show* for a picture book was remarkable. This was my first autographing; we were sitting at two tiny tables, like school desks, and Jim was on one side and I was on the other. He had a line going out the door, up the street, and I had two polite people who took pity on me and bought my book. I watched in awe as people paid their respects to Jim.

After this was over, I was lucky enough to walk through Boston Common with him. He was so kind and generous to somebody starting out and encouraged me to "stick with it." As we were saying our goodbyes, he said, "Marc, don't ever tell anyone how easy it is, what we do." I said, "Jim, it's not easy!"

A couple of years later we both spoke at the Massachusetts School of Art. I remember him standing in the space; he wasn't a tall man, but he had such a command of the room. He was so generous with these art students, telling them what he knew about creating children's books. He was always encouraging others. Artists, of course, work in isolation, but Jim gave of himself and shared whenever he came out of the studio.

I was sitting in Walter Lorraine's office right after Jim delivered the art for *Miss Nelson Is Missing!* Walter asked me if I wanted to see Jim's new book. I looked at it and thought it brilliant.

There is no one who can write a better, sharper, more concise line of dialogue. He could establish a character with so few words. I work so hard at distilling the words I use in my books to get that right balance between what the words do and what the pictures do. Jim had such a gift for that.

I did correspond with him during his illness, before his death. I was at a little bed-and-breakfast in Maine when I opened the *New York Times* and saw his obituary. I knew his death was coming, but it was still so sad. He died much too young. He gave so much joy and comfort to so many families and children. Jim Marshall was one of the true geniuses of the children's book world.

Jacket art © 1985 by Marc Brown

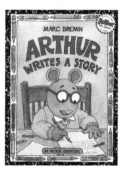

Jacket art © 1998 by Marc Brown

MARC BROWN's award-winning books about Arthur and his world have become international bestsellers and have been made into an Emmy Award—winning television series on PBS. He gets much of his inspiration for his books from real life—from his own children and the children he meets. Splitting his time between his homes in Martha's Vineyard and New York City, he lives with his wife, the critically acclaimed author and illustrator Laurie Krasny Brown.

FIVE STORIES

ABOUT

TWO DEAR FRIENDS

✤

STORY NUMBER ONE

THE BOX

Martha noticed a little box

on George's kitchen table.

"Do not open," said the sign.

"I won't," said Martha.

"I'm not the nosy type."

But Martha couldn't take her eyes off

the little box.

She read the sign again.

"Do not open," said the sign.

Martha couldn't stand it.

"One little peek won't hurt," she said.

And she untied the string.

Out jumped George's entire collection of

Mexican jumping beans.

"Oh my stars," said Martha.

It took Martha all afternoon to
round up the Mexican jumping beans.
One yellow one gave her quite a chase.

When George came home

Martha was reading a magazine.

"You seem out of breath," said George.

"You don't think I opened that little box,

 do you?" said Martha.

"Of course not," said George.

"I'm not the nosy type," said Martha.

George didn't say a word.

STORY NUMBER TWO
THE HIGH BOARD

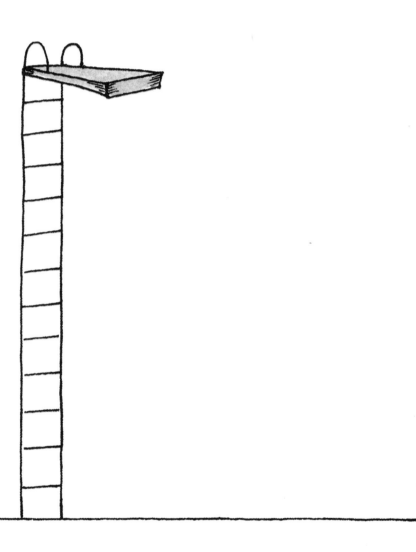

"Today," said George, "I will jump from
the high board!"

"Don't do it!" cried Martha.

"Everyone will be watching!" said George.

"You'd never catch *me* up there!" said Martha.

"That's because you're a scaredy-cat," said George.

But when George got up on the high board,

he lost his nerve.

"I can't do it," he said.

"And everyone is watching!"

His knees began to shake.

"I'll be right up," said Martha.

Martha climbed up the ladder.

"Now what?" said George.

"I'll go first," said Martha.

And she jumped off.

Martha caused quite a splash.

Everyone was impressed.

And no one noticed how George got down.

"I just didn't feel like it today," said George.

Martha didn't say a word.

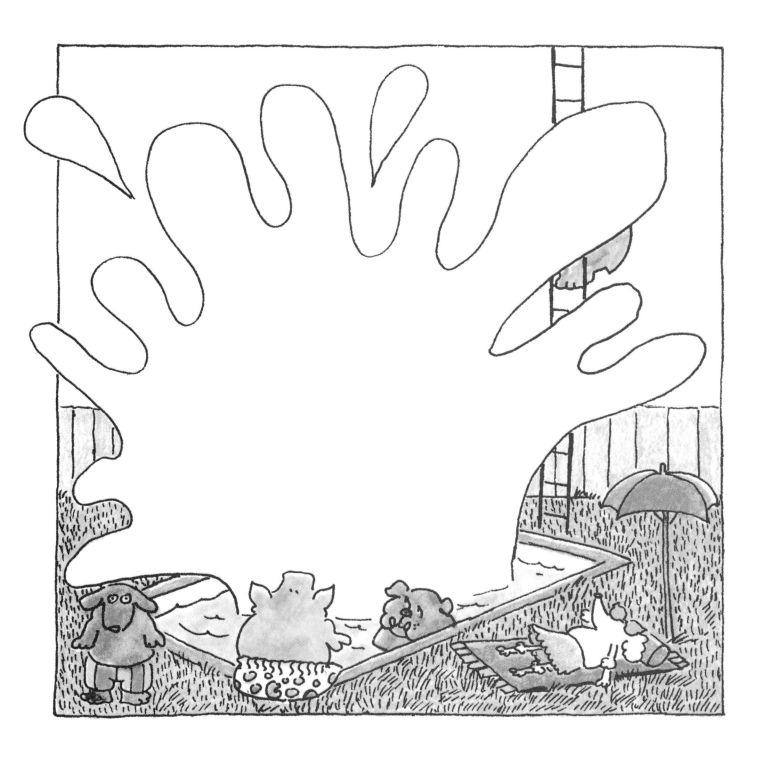

STORY NUMBER THREE

THREE

THE TRICK

George was fond of playing tricks on Martha.

But that was not Martha's idea of fun.

And when she found her house slippers

nailed to the floor, she was not amused.

Martha gave George the old

silent treatment.

"Oh no!" said George. "Not that!"

George decided to bake Martha's favorite cake.

"This will butter her up," he said.

When the cake was done,

George put it in a box.

And he went to look for a pretty ribbon.

"I have a surprise for you," said George.

"It's another trick!" said Martha.

"Not this time," said George.

"Then *you* open it," said Martha.

"Very well," said George. "I will."

Martha bit her nails, while George
pulled off the ribbon.

Out jumped one rubber tarantula,

one stuffed snake, four plastic spiders,

and two real frogs!

"Egads!" cried George. "I've been tricked!"

"And by the way," said Martha.

"The cake was simply delicious."

George was excited about his new job.

"It's hard work," said Martha.

"You must be *very* strict."

"I'll try," said George.

"No horsing around is allowed!"
said Martha.

"Thanks for the advice," said George.

"That's what friends are for,"
said Martha.

Very soon George saw that someone
was disobeying the rules.

"No horsing around!" he called through
his megaphone.

"It's all right!" shouted Martha.

"It's only me!"

"You heard me!" called out George.

George meant business.

And he gave Martha quite a bawling out.

"Well!" said Martha,

"And I thought we were friends!"

"Oh dear," said George. "Martha was right —

this *is* a hard job!"

THE LAST STORY

THE BOOK

George was all nice and cozy.

"May I join you?" said Martha.

"I'm reading," said George.

"I'll be as quiet as a mouse," said Martha.

"Thank you," said George.

And he went back to his book.

But soon Martha was fidgeting.

"Please!" said George.

"Have some consideration!"

"Sorry," said Martha.

George went back to his reading.

But in no time Martha was fidgeting again.

"That does it!" said George.

And he left.

At home he got all nice and cozy again.

He opened his book.

"It is important to be considerate
to our friends," said the book.

"It certainly *is!*" said George.

"Sometimes we are thoughtless without even
knowing it," said the book.

"*I'll* say!" said George.

"Martha should read this book."

He went to find her.

"I'm sorry I was fidgeting," said Martha.

"I got lonely."

"Oh," said George. "I never considered that."

"What did you want to tell me?" said Martha.

"Oh nothing," said George.

"I just got lonely too."

And they sat and told stories into the night.

Martha didn't fidget even once.

Coleen Salley

HE WAS MARTHA, AND I WAS GEORGE

JIM AND I BECAME GOOD FRIENDS BASICALLY BECAUSE HE HAD A TERRIBLE FEAR OF FLYING. He traveled by train to see his mother, going from New York to San Antonio. Therefore, he came through New Orleans on the Southern Bell and then he took another train to San Antonio. He loved New Orleans, where I live, so he would spend some time here, and we'd go to great restaurants for dinner. Consequently, I saw him more than if we had just been at the same conferences together. We had the same sort of humor. I always likened us to George and Martha. But he was Martha, and I was George. Jim had his feet on the ground; he had such a gentle, sweet sense of humor. I was the goofy one!

Jim didn't graduate from one of the prestigious art schools, like the Rhode Island School of Design or Parsons. Everyone he associated with did. He always felt self-conscious, as if he didn't have the right credentials. I felt the same way. I had become a full professor at University of New Orleans and didn't have a Ph.D. So we identified with each other. That is one of the reasons his friendship with Maurice Sendak was so important to him. Maurice really appreciated Jim and his art. That gave Jim reassurance about his worth as a children's book creator.

Jim was devoted to his mother, Cecille Marshall. She was a beautiful southern lady, petite and always impeccably dressed. Jim was so good to her; he did anything that he could do to make her life easier. A generous, thoughtful son, he took her places; he set her up in the best hotels when she traveled.

Jim loved Marathon, Texas. As a boy he spent summers there with his grandfather. It is a small little town with shops, artists' studios, and an old hotel. He wanted to be buried in Marathon. The town fathers were planning to tear down an old windmill that was in the cemetery. Jim bought the windmill, a memory of his childhood. He was buried under it, and Cecille placed a headstone commemorating Jim and some of his characters.

Jim's death had been heartbreaking for Cecille. I wanted to support her emotionally, so I drove over to San Antonio so that she and I could visit Jim's grave in Marathon. They had had a huge rainstorm the week before we arrived. The whole cemetery was abloom with wildflowers, and Cecille was absolutely stunned. She'd had no idea that there were any plants in the cemetery, which is located in a high desert terrain. She didn't know that all those wildflowers seeds were there, under the surface, waiting for some water to help them pop out. It was awesome that we came on that particular day.

Even though he has been dead for many years, Jim and his work have not faded away. Miss Nelson and George and Martha are now part of the canon of children's literature. I'm so pleased that those children's book seeds he planted many years ago continue to bloom year after year, just like the wildflowers by his grave.

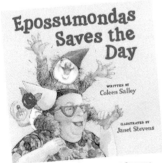

Jacket art © 2006 by Janet Stevens

Jacket art © 2004 by Janet Stevens

COLEEN SALLEY is an author, storyteller, and retired professor of children's literature. Her books for children include Epossumondas and Who's That Tripping Over My Bridge?, and she has toured the United States and the entire world as a professional storyteller. She was a professor at the University of New Orleans, and a visiting professor at numerous colleges and universities around the country. She lives in the French Quarter in New Orleans, Louisiana, and has become a staple at the Mardi Gras festivities there.

FIVE STORIES ABOUT
THE BEST OF FRIENDS

STORY NUMBER ONE

THE CLOCK

George gave Martha a present

for her birthday.

"It's a cuckoo clock," said George.

"So I see," said Martha.

"It's nice and loud," said George.

"So I hear," said Martha.

"Do you like it?" asked George.

"Oh yes indeed," said Martha.

But to tell the truth,

the cuckoo clock got on Martha's nerves.

The next day

George went to Martha's house.

Martha was not at home.

And the cuckoo clock

was not on the wall.

"Maybe she likes it so much

she took it with her," said George.

Just then he heard a faint

"Cuckoo… cuckoo… cuckoo."

To George's surprise,

the cuckoo clock was at the bottom

of Martha's laundry basket.

When Martha returned,

she couldn't look George in the eye.

"It must have fallen in by mistake,"

she said. "I do hope it isn't broken."

"Not at all," said George.

"The paint isn't even chipped,

the clock works just dandy,

and the cuckoo hasn't lost

its splendid voice."

"Would you like to borrow it?"

asked Martha.

George was delighted.

He found just the right spot for it, too.

Wasn't that considerate of

Martha to lend me her clock? thought George.

"Cuckoo," said the clock.

STORY NUMBER TWO

THE TRIP

George invited Martha

on an ocean cruise.

"Is *this* the boat?" said Martha.

"Use your imagination," said George.

"I'll try," said Martha.

Very soon it was raining cats and dogs.

"This is unpleasant," said Martha.

"Use your imagination," said George.

"Think of it as a thrilling storm

at sea."

"I'll try," said Martha.

"Lunch is served," said George.

And he gave Martha a soggy cracker.

Martha was not impressed.

"Use your imagination," said George.

"Oh looky," said Martha.

"What a pretty shark."

"A shark!" cried George.

George took a spill.

"But where's the shark?" he said.

"Really," said Martha.

"You must learn to use
your imagination."

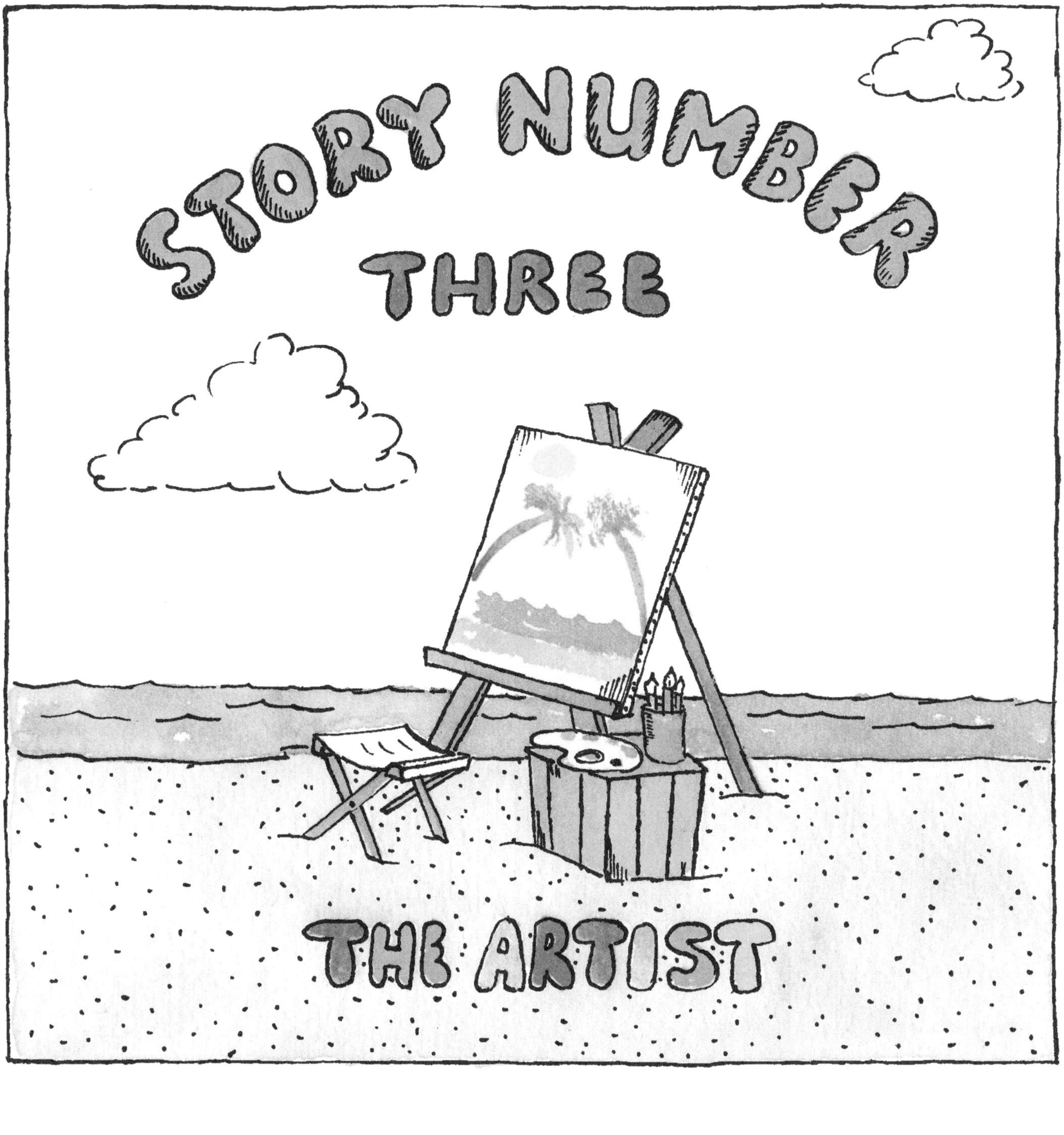
STORY NUMBER
THREE
THE ARTIST

George was painting in oils.

"That ocean doesn't look right," said Martha.

"Add some more blue.

And that sand looks all wrong.

Add a bit more yellow."

"Please," said George.

"Artists don't like interference."

But Martha just couldn't help herself.

"Those palm trees look funny," she said.

"That does it!" said George.

"See if you can do better!"

And he went off in a huff.

"My, my," said Martha.

"Some artists are *so* touchy."

And she began to make

a few little improvements.

When George returned

Martha proudly displayed the painting.

George was flabbergasted.

"You've ruined it!" he cried.

"I'm sorry you feel that way," said Martha.

"I like it."

Martha was one of those artists

who aren't a bit touchy.

STORY NUMBER FOUR

THE ATTIC

One cold and stormy night

George decided to peek into the attic.

"Go on up," said Martha.

"Oooh no," said George.

"There might be a ghost up there,

or a skeleton, or a vampire,

or maybe even some werewolves."

"Oooh goody!" said Martha.

"Let's investigate!"

But there wasn't much to see in the attic,

only a box of old rubber bands.

George was disappointed.

"Would you like to hear a story

that will give you goose bumps?" asked Martha.

"You bet," said George.

"When you hear it, your bones will go cold,"

said Martha.

"Oooh," said George.

"Your blood will curdle," said Martha.

"Ooooh," said George.

"And you'll feel mummy fingers

up and down your spine," said Martha.

"Stop!" cried George. "I can't take any more.

Tell me some other time!"

That night Martha went to bed
with the light on.
She had a bad case of goose bumps.

One late-summer morning

George had a wicked idea.

"I shouldn't," he said.

"I really shouldn't."

But he just couldn't help himself.

"Here comes the rain!" he cried.

"Egads!" screamed Martha.

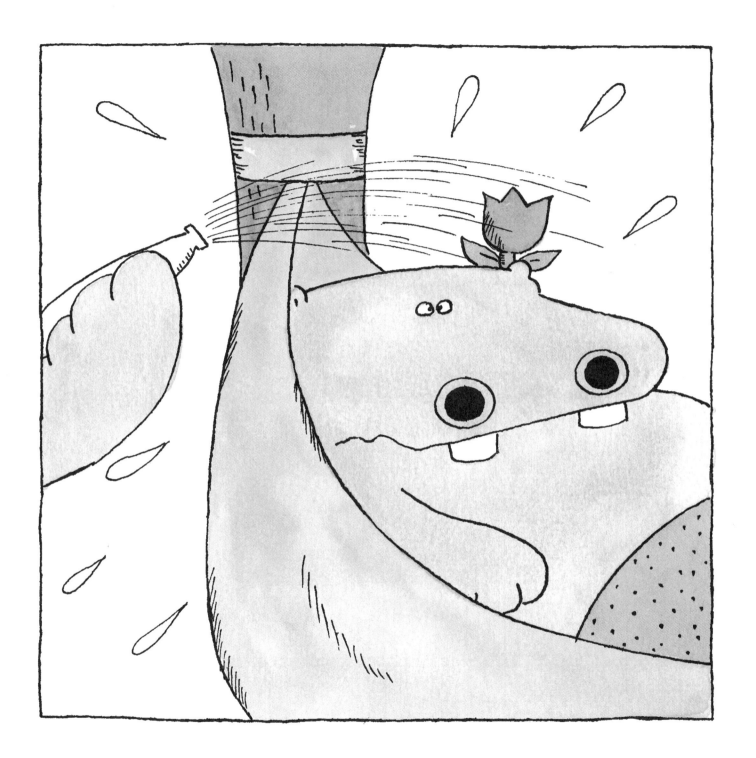

Martha was thoroughly drenched

and as mad as a wet hen.

"That did it!" she said.

"We are no longer on speaking terms!"

"I was only horsing around,"

said George.

But Martha was unmoved.

The next morning, Martha read a funny story.

"I can't wait to tell George," she said.

Then she remembered that she and George

were no longer on speaking terms.

Around noon Martha heard a joke on the radio.

"George will love this one," she said.

But she and George weren't speaking.

In the afternoon Martha observed

the first autumn leaf fall to the ground.

"Autumn is George's favorite season," she said.

Another leaf came swirling down.

"That does it," said Martha.

Martha went straight to George's house.

"I forgive you," she said.

George was delighted to be back
on speaking terms.

"Good friends just can't stay cross
for long," said George.

"You can say that again,"
said Martha.

And together they watched the
autumn arrive.

But when summer rolled around again,
Martha was ready and waiting.

Afterword

Born in San Antonio, Texas, in 1942, James Marshall never planned to become a children's book author. He played the viola and attended the New England Conservatory of Music until a physical accident ended his career. He then studied French and history, received a master's degree from Trinity College, and taught French and Spanish at the high school level.

Although without any formal art instruction, Jim still loved to doodle, placing eyes and lines together to fashion a character. One day, lying in a hammock in San Antonio, he found himself sketching two intriguing hippos. On the radio he had been listening to Edward Albee's play *Who's Afraid of*

Virginia Woolf? and hence named these characters George and Martha.

Jim's children's book career began when his friend Laurette Murdock, who worked in Houghton Mifflin's copyediting department, suggested that he meet with Houghton's children's book publisher, Walter Lorraine. Jim brought two undeveloped books with him, *What's the Matter with Carruthers?* and *George and Martha.* Walter Lorraine had a legendary eye for talent and over his career signed on the first books of David Macaulay, Lois Lowry, Chris Van Allsburg, Jack Gantos, Nicole Rubel, and Susan Meddaugh, to name only a few. Because Walter sensed that Jim really needed work, he gave him a book to illustrate, Byrd Baylor's *Plink, Plink, Plink,* until Jim had time to complete one of his own.

James Marshall titled this loving 1991 tribute to his cat Marcel *Seven-Part Portrait of Marcel*—one cat, seven poses, with Marshall's home in Mansfield, Connecticut, as backdrop.

Since Jim needed to learn how to create art for a book, Walter became a coach in the illustration process, one often fraught with difficulty. Most of the George and Martha books, except the last, were executed in the four-color overlay process. That meant Jim had to do by hand what later illustrators would rely on the camera to accomplish. So for each page in the book, Jim made four different drawings, one for each color: for a 48-page book he had to execute 192 pieces of art.

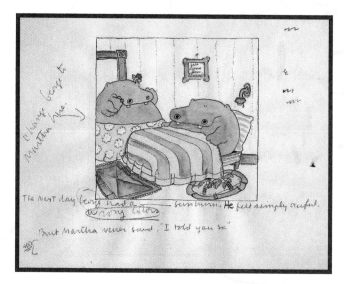 

Jim grew more skilled as an illustrator with each book, but he was always gifted when it came to content. In an interview in 2007, Walter Lorraine said, "Right from the start I knew he had a lot to offer. He was so imaginative and creative even in those rough dummies. Although he lacked experience technically, conceptually he was superior. *George and Martha* contains one of the best statements about relationships that I have ever seen, including in any adult bestseller. He sums it up in a few lines and words—pea soup in the loafers."

Working with Jim on these books was a dynamic process, an enormous amount of fun for everyone involved. Jim once drew a story on a cocktail napkin. Walter said, "I'll publish that" and did. Many details came out of office discussion. In *The Stupids Die* the line "This isn't heaven. . . . This is Cleveland," emerged as Jim and Walter threw lines back and forth in conversation. However, Jim frequently missed his deadlines for the final delivery of a book. "He was a great storyteller personally as well. His grandmother died three times, according to Jim, to explain overdue artwork." One day Walter commandeered one of the Houghton Mifflin offices, put Jim in the room, and shut the door behind him. A few hours later he emerged with his overdue book, and everyone's frowns turned to smiles.

Sue Sherman, art director at Houghton Mifflin in the 1980s, remembers with fondness the joy of working with Jim on a book. He would come in with a bunch of pictures and they would pick the best one. "He'd do two or three versions, and then let us choose. He wasn't always clear about how the story would go." In one rendition of "The Beach," George gets a sunburn; in another, Martha turns red. While talking about the story, Jim eventually worked out the best plot. Because he always kept the creation process so spontaneous, nothing seems strained or overworked in his books. It is so easy for a picture book to get the life beat out of it. Editors look at it; art directors raise questions; many people present opinions. Jim's creative process kept everything fluid. All of his sketches look as if he had just tossed them off—in large part because he waited as long as he could to produce his final art.

His creative process can today be observed in his notebooks, available at the University of Connecticut in Storrs, the Kerlan Collection in Minneapolis, Minnesota, and the de Grummond

The next day Martha had a terrible sunburn!
She felt all hot and itchy.
But George never said "I told you so."
Because that's not what friends are for.

Top left: James Marshall's initial sketches from "The Beach," initially with a sunburned George.

This page: The finished illustration—Martha has the sunburn.

Collection in Hattesburg, Mississippi. Usually he nailed the basic essence of each book on the first draft. But then he simplified, making the lines funnier and the situations subtler. As Jim revised, he concentrated on finding more humor: "monkey business" became "horsing around"; "favorite cake" was replaced with "favorite goodies"; "She'll be pleasantly surprised" turned into "This will butter her up." He added dramatic tension to the drawings. In the first drafts of "The High Board," George stands alone on the diving board and Martha and others can be seen on the ground. The later illustration features George solo, looking precarious, as if he will fall at any moment.

James Marshall hard at work in "real life."

Maurice Sendak's essay in this book mentions Jim's "delicate sense of restraint." Jim's touch actually grew lighter as each book progressed. Anything heavy-handed was eliminated; the story began to happen between the lines. If Jim had originally sketched out a moral, it vanished. In its place, he substituted a more ambiguous phrase, such as "George didn't say a word." Jim trusted children. He knew they could bring their own intelligence to stories; he gave them room for their own imaginations.

In the 1970s and 1980s, after the publication of each book, I had an opportunity to travel with Jim as he interacted with these children and his multitude of adult fans while he spoke in bookstores,

James Marshall's self-portrait of himself working on a train during a Chicago snowstorm.

schools, and libraries, and at conferences. Although children's book authors today often go on book tours, Jim served as one of the pioneers in that arena. No one kept this kind of travel livelier. Always funny, always slightly irreverent, he remained amazingly attuned to those around him. Now having spent more than a decade as an author myself on just such tours, I am even more amazed at how sensitive Jim could be to the needs of others while the spotlight shone on him. Book tours tend to make the best human beings self-absorbed and self-centered. Not Jim.

One afternoon when we were supposed to meet the *Los Angeles Times* book reviewer Barbara Karlin, who had just been hospitalized, Jim immediately took charge of the situation; sushi and a hospital visit were in order. Several of Barbara's friends came with us, and we were almost evicted for our raucous laughter. Later Jim helped Barbara financially, because she had expensive medical treatments, by securing for her a book contract, *Cinderella*, which they worked on together. The word "generous" pales in comparison to how he lived his life.

The potbelly stove and other exquisite elements of James Marshall's Mansfield, Connecticut, home.

Jim in turn cared for and doted on his mother, his sister, his partner, Bill Gray, his multitude of friends, and even those who worked for his publishers. He provided temporary housing for Walter Lorraine. At one point in my life, after the suicide of a close friend left me emotionally vulnerable, Jim whisked me off to his home in Connecticut and took care of me as only he could. His house in Mansfield, with a picket fence and flower beds, looked just like George and Martha's home: a tiny cottage with a potbelly stove, very cozy, and everything, including Japanese chests, exquisite. Like his famous protagonists, he never made a big deal about being a friend. He simply spent his life and energy being one.

The last time I saw Jim, we were in San Antonio. He hired a cab, and then we stopped in the neighborhood where he grew up, his school, and his favorite places as a child and adult. We both knew that he was very ill; consequently, we talked about his childhood, his accidental but satisfying career as an author, and his hopes that the books would endure.

Published more than fifteen years after his death, this volume affirms the resiliency of his work. "I like the George and Martha books. They make me happy," a first-grader once wrote to Jim. These sunny stories still make us smile. Jim Marshall wrote the best books about friendship and invented some of the most lovable characters in the canon of children's literature. Decades after the appearance of *George and Martha* in 1972, his picture books attest to his incredible ability to communicate with children—and his own personal genius for friendship.

Anita Silvey
WESTWOOD, MASSACHUSETTS